The Beavers' Busy Year

by Mary Holland

Did you know that beavers are mammals just like you? They have some hair, the mothers produce milk for their young, and most give birth to live young.

Beavers are a kind of mammal called a rodent. Mice, chipmunks, squirrels, woodchucks, and porcupines are also rodents. They all have four big front teeth called incisors that never stop growing. Can you find the incisors in the skull above?

Beavers use their incisors to cut down trees, to cut the trees into pieces, and to eat the bark. This helps to keep their incisors from growing too long.

They do most of this work at night, while you are sleeping, and they sleep during the day.

Beavers are good recyclers. They chew and eat the bark off sticks. Then the beavers use the sticks to build a dam across a stream. The dam stops the water from flowing, and turns the stream into a pond.

Beavers also use sticks to build a home called a lodge. They make a pile of sticks and mud on the bottom of the pond that is so big, it pokes up out of the water.

Then the beavers chew a room inside the pile of sticks. The room is always above water and dry. This is where the beavers live.

Each lodge usually has more than one door or entrance. The doors to a lodge are underwater so many of the beavers' enemies (like coyotes and wolves) can't get to them.

Beavers spend a lot of time in the water. In addition to having thick fur that keeps them warm, beavers have valves in their ears and noses that close when they go underwater.

Beavers have special, see-through eyelids that serve as goggles when they go underwater. When swimming, beavers steer with their tail and paddle with their webbed, hind feet.

In the fall, beavers get ready for winter. They are very busy adding sticks and mud to their dam and lodge. They also gather a supply of food. Beavers cut down trees and make a pile of branches in the pond near their lodge. They will eat from this pile when the pond is iced over.

Beavers spend a lot of time in their dark, lodge in the winter. Sometimes there can be ten or more beavers living in one lodge.

Once ice forms on top of the pond, the beavers cannot get onto land to cut down any more trees. They swim to their food pile under the ice and carry branches back to the lodge to eat.

As the weather warms and the ice thins, the beavers use their heads to bump through the ice. Then they can see the sun and eat fresh bark once again.

In the spring, the mother beaver gives birth to between two and four baby beavers, called kits. Later in the summer, the kits go outside the lodge with their parents.

Kits live with their parents until they turn two years old. Then they leave the lodge to find a mate and a stream that they can turn into their own pond.

When summer comes there are lots of green plants for beavers to eat.

They work on their lodge and dam in the spring and fall, so there isn't much heavy work for beavers to do in the summer.

When beavers aren't eating or swimming, they are often grooming themselves and each other. They usually groom with their feet. The two inside toenails on a beaver's hind foot are split. Beavers use these nails to comb through tangled fur and to rub oil from their bodies into their fur to make it waterproof. Sometimes they use these nails to remove splinters from between their teeth.

When fall arrives again, the beavers dive back into their work in order to get ready for winter.

For Creative Minds

Beaver Signs

Just because you don't see beavers, doesn't mean that they aren't there. Beavers live near water in cities and in the country and sleep during the day (nocturnal). While you may not see the beavers themselves, you might see signs that beavers are near. Match the descriptions of the beaver signs (in bold) to the images (by number).

Beaver families build their home, called a **lodge**, by piling sticks on the bottom of a pond. Sometimes beavers build their lodge on the banks of a pond, not in the middle of it. If you see a pile of sticks on the banks of a pond, you are probably spotting a beaver lodge. If the sticks are blocking the flow of the water and turning a stream into a pond, it's a beaver dam.

Have you ever left bite marks on something? When beavers eat the bark off a tree trunk, they turn their heads sideways and bring their four incisors together. Each tooth makes an **incisor bite mark** in the wood.

When beavers first live in a pond, they cut down trees close to their lodge and dam. Eventually they have to go farther and farther to find trees. Beavers are safer in water than they are on land because they can swim much faster than they can run. They dig ditches or canals that fill with water so the beavers can swim to the far-away trees and float them back to the lodge. If you see ditches or canals going from ponds into nearby meadows or woods, you are probably seeing a **beaver canal**.

Beavers are territorial. Like dogs and many other animals, they mark their home area with smells or scents. The beavers build piles of mud and leaves beside the pond. Then they spread a strong-smelling oily liquid called castoreum on the pile. These piles are called **scent mounds**. There are many messages the scent may be giving to other beavers, including "stay away" or "I'm looking for a mate."

Answers: 1-scent mound, 2-beaver canal, 3-lodge, 4-incisor bite marks

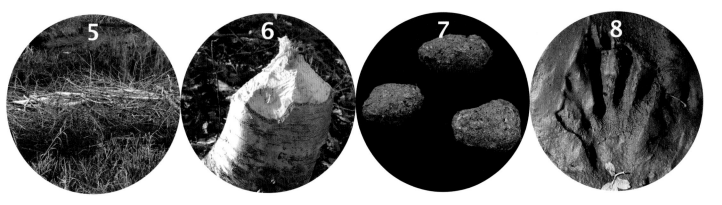

Have you ever left footprints on a clean floor or in dirt? Beaver **tracks** are the same shape as their feet. The tracks made by a beaver's front feet are small, and the tracks from its webbed hind feet are large. While some tracks are very clear, others may be rubbed out by dragging their tail or wood. You might find beaver tracks in the mud at the edge of a beaver pond. Sometimes, you might even find tracks in snow.

If beavers are living in a pond, there will be lots of trees that have been cut down for food and for building a dam and a lodge. There will also be many wood chips on the ground by these tree stumps. The beavers chew the chips off the tree trunks in order to make the trees fall down. When beavers cut down a tree with their incisors, it leaves a **pointed tree-trunk tip**.

Beavers keep their lodge very clean and only go to the bathroom in the water. You don't see their droppings, or **scat**, very often. Look for it in the water near their dam. Beaver scat is about as long as your pinkie finger, and it is made of little bits of bark that look like sawdust.

Before ice forms on the pond, beavers cut down branches and put them in a **food-supply pile** on the bottom of the pond near their lodge. When the pond is frozen with ice and they can't leave the pond to get food, they swim out to this pile of branches to get food to eat. After they take a branch or piece of log back to the lodge, they eat it, and then throw the leftovers back into the pond.

More Beaver Signs:

bank lodge   floating food leftovers   chewed bark   beaver dam

Answers: 5-winter food-supply pile, 6-pointed tree trunk, 7-scat, 8-hind foot track

Beavers as Habitat Engineers

Beaver Lodge in Pond   Abandoned Beaver Lodge

Other than humans, no other creature changes its surroundings as much as beavers. They turn small, wooded streams into ponds, and turn forests into open meadows. The new ponds and meadows become habitats for fish, birds, and many other animals.

First, they must choose just the right size stream—not too small and not too large.

Next, they build a strong dam to limit the flow of the stream enough to raise the water level. Sticks, branches, logs, stones, mud, and plants are used to build the dam. The shape and size of the dam depends on where it is built. The upstream side of a dam is usually much longer than the downstream side, which makes it very strong. Dams blocking larger streams are often bowed upstream, as that also adds strength to the dam.

Then the beavers build a lodge in the bank or in the middle of the pond. Beavers rely on the water around their lodges to protect them from their enemies (predators) like coyotes and wolves. The doors to the lodges are underwater because most of their enemies don't swim. The beavers have several underwater doors going in and out of their lodge so they can easily escape from danger.

Beavers are always checking on the water level of their pond. Some water still flows through the dam, but it is very important that the entrances to the beaver lodge stay under water. This keeps predators from reaching the beavers when they are inside the lodge. If the water gets too low because the dam is leaking, the beavers are quick to repair the dam.

After several years, when the beavers have eaten all the food close to the pond, they look for another stream where there is more food and build a new pond. Without the beavers there to tend it, the dam weakens and cannot hold back the pond water. When the old dam breaks, the pond drains, turns into a marsh, and then into a meadow with a stream running through it. In time, shrubs and trees may grow where the pond used to be, making a forest once again.

Dam Building

Beavers need deep water around their lodges to keep predators away. The beavers don't go to the local hardware store to buy what they need; they have to find things in the area around where they are building.

If they need branches, they cut trees and then cut the branches. They don't have saws to cut the wood, so they use their long incisor teeth.

If they need mud, they find it and dig it. Beavers don't have shovels, so they use their hand-like front feet and strong, claw-like nails to help them dig.

They gather other things in their habitat to use in the dam. These other items might be plants or even trash left by humans. Hopefully, the trash won't hurt them.

After they find things to use in the dam, they have to carry the items to the building site. They can carry things in their teeth and in their front paws—even when swimming!

Once they get the items back to the dam-building site, they still have to pile it so that it stays together with the water pushing against it.

Even after the dam is built, the beavers work hard to keep it in good shape—until it is time to leave the area and build a new beaver pond somewhere else.

Which of these things do you think beavers might use to build a dam?

Answers: All of them: sticks, fishing float, mud, and stones.

Keystone Animal: Beaver Pond Wildlife

Some people think that beavers are "pests" because the beavers cut down their trees or turn their backyard into a beaver pond. Scientists who study beavers have shown us that beavers are a **keystone species**. That means that many other plants and animals depend on beaver ponds and wetlands. When the beavers leave to build a new pond, some of the other living things may completely disappear from the area.

Which of these animals do you think would rely on beaver ponds and wetlands for all or some of their needs?

Answer: All of these animals live in and around the beaver pond. Starting in the upper left, animals are: eastern newt, wood duck, painted turtles, moose, green frog, red-winged blackbird, river otter, green heron, snapping turtle, white-tailed deer, raccoon, dragonfly, and great blue heron.

Beaver Tails

Beavers are easily identified by their long, flat tails that are covered with scales.

Beavers slap their tails on the water to signal danger to other beavers.

They also store fat in their tails during the winter, which helps them survive. When it's hot outside in the summer, the tails release heat, helping to keep the beavers cool.

Beavers use their tails for balance and to support standing—like a bike kickstand.

Last but not least, beavers use their tails as rudders to steer while swimming and for balance when floating in the water.

For more information on beaver adaptations, go to the free on-line teaching activities at SylvanDellPublishing.com. Click on the book's cover to get to its homepage.

This book would not have been possible without the generosity, patience and devotion of Kay Shumway, a beaver whisperer if there ever was one—MH

Thanks to Chiho Kaneko for the use of her Beaver lodge illustration.

Thanks to Amy Yeakel, Education Program Director, and Dave Erler, Senior Naturalist, at the Squam Lakes Natural Science Center for verifying the accuracy of the information in this book.

El ocupadísimo año de los castores: Title in Spanish, translated by Rosalyna Toth

Library of Congress Cataloging-in-Publication Data

Holland, Mary, 1946- author.
  The beavers' busy year / by Mary Holland.
     pages cm
  Audience: 4-8.
  Audience: Grade K to 3.
  ISBN 978-1-62855-204-1 (English hardcover) -- ISBN 978-1-62855-213-3 (English pbk.) -- ISBN 978-1-62855-231-7 (English downloadable ebook) -- ISBN 978-1-62855-249-2 (English interactive) -- ISBN 978-1-62855-222-5 (Spanish pbk.) -- ISBN 978-1-62855-240-9 (Spanish downloadable ebook) -- ISBN 978-1-62855-258-4 (Spanish interactive)
  1. Beavers--Juvenile literature. 2. Beavers--Habitations--Juvenile literature. I. Title.
  QL737.R632H65 2014
  599.37--dc23
                           2013036382

Lexile® Level: 940

key phrases for educators: adaptations, change
environment, habitat interaction, seasons

Copyright 2014 © by Mary Holland

The "For Creative Minds" educational section may
be copied by the owner for personal use or by
educators using copies in classroom settings

Manufactured in China, December 2013
This product conforms to CPSIA 2008
First Printing

Sylvan Dell Publishing
Mt. Pleasant, SC 29464
www.SylvanDellPublishing.com